EGMONT
We bring stories to life

First published in Great Britain 2012 by Dean,
an imprint of Egmont UK Limited
239 Kensington High Street, London W8 6SA

ISBN 978 0 6035 6678 3
51290/1
Printed in China

Joker Soaker

It was a very hot day in Pontypandy and the village was suffering from a drought.

Dilys was mopping the steps outside her shop, when she noticed a parcel.

"Looks like a present from your Uncle Dylan in Newtown!" Dilys called to her son, Norman.

Norman went outside, grabbed the parcel and peeked inside. He dashed back into the shop and ripped open the box.

"Cool! A Joker Soaker!" Norman cried.

When Dilys' back was turned, Norman filled up the water pistol from his mum's mop bucket.

"Now to find my first victim," Norman sniggered.

He spotted Tom Thomas in his rescue jeep. Norman aimed his water pistol at the car's open window, blasting Tom with water!

"Flamin' koalas!" Tom exclaimed.

"Bull's eye!" laughed Norman, before he felt a tap on his shoulder. It was Fireman Sam.

Quickly, Norman dashed off with the Joker Soaker before Sam could confiscate it.

Over in Pontypandy Park, Dusty was feeling very hot and thirsty.

In the distance, he saw Helen Flood and Trevor Evans talking on the other side of the railings.

"I've never known it so dry!" complained Trevor, mopping his brow with a handkerchief. "Not enough water to wash my bus!"

"I've been buying bottled water from the shop!" Helen nodded in agreement.

Dusty noticed the bottle of water in Helen's shopping basket and crept closer to the pair.

Dusty pushed his head through the railings behind Helen. He tried to grab the bottle of water between his teeth but couldn't quite reach.

Dusty stretched his head further through the railings, but Trevor and Helen hadn't noticed him and walked away.

Realising the bottle of water had gone, Dusty tried to pull his head back through the railings but it wouldn't fit.

Dusty was stuck!

Back in the village, Sarah and James were eating ice creams. "I wish it would rain to cool me down!" sighed Sarah.

Suddenly, a stream of water splashed all over Sarah's head!

It was Naughty Norman with his water pistol!

"Joker's the name, soaking's my game!" laughed Norman.

But as he went to squirt the twins again, Norman realised the gun was empty.

He raced off with the twins chasing after him.

As Norman was running past the Fire Station, he spotted a pipe outside. Norman quickly filled up his water pistol just as Sarah and James appeared.

"There he is!" shouted James. "Come back!"

But Norman was too quick for the twins.

A little later on, Norman reached the park. He saw Dusty by the railings.

Norman raised his Joker Soaker and aimed it at the dog.

"Right, Dusty!" cried Norman. "Reach for the sky!"

But before Norman could squirt Dusty, the dog slumped to the ground.

"Dusty? Are you all right?" asked Norman. Dusty's tongue was hanging out and he was panting hard.

"Golly, you're well and truly stuck," realised Norman. "And you look really thirsty! I'll fix that."

He gently lifted Dusty's head and squirted a few drops of water into the dog's mouth.

Sarah and James arrived. Sarah tried to take the Joker Soaker away from Norman.

"We're going to hand this over to Uncle Sam," said James. "This is the last time you waste water in hot weather!"

"No, don't! I need it for Dusty!" cried Norman. "Just look at him . . ."

The twins saw how ill Dusty looked and realised that the dog was in danger.

"We've got to get him out of here!" cried Sarah. "Let's call Uncle Sam."

At the Fire Station, Fireman Sam received the call. "Dog in distress?" he read. "We'll soon sort that!"

Fireman Sam, Penny and Elvis quickly climbed into Jupiter. They raced off, sirens blaring!

When the crew arrived, the children explained what had happened.

"Bring me the grease, please Elvis," said Sam. "We'll try to ease him out first."

Dusty whimpered as Elvis covered the dog's ears in grease. Sam tried to gently release Dusty from the railings, but he was still stuck.

"I think we're going to need the Jaws of Life," said Fireman Sam.

Elvis fetched the metal-cutting tool from Jupiter and gave it to Fireman Sam.

As Sam approached the railings, poor Dusty began to whimper even more loudly.

"Easy, boy," said Sam, stroking Dusty's fur. "I won't hurt you!"

Using the Jaws of Life, Sam quickly cut through one of the railings. Elvis bent the metal back to give Dusty enough room to escape.

"Well done, Sam!" cried Sarah. The twins and Norman cheered!

But Dusty wasn't out of danger yet. He needed a drink of water quickly.

Fireman Sam filled up a bucket with water from a tap on the side of the fire engine.

"There you go, boy," said Sam, setting the bucket in front of Dusty. The dog lapped up the water and was soon feeling much better.

Norman began to sneak away.

"Not so fast, Norman Price!" cried Sam. "I haven't forgotten those tricks you've been playing."

"Sorry, Sam," said a sheepish Norman.

"But since you came to Dusty's rescue," smiled Fireman Sam, "I'm going to forget it just this once."

"Thanks, Sam," said Norman.

"That's quite a gadget you've got there," continued Sam. "Can I take a look?"

Norman handed Fireman Sam the water pistol.

"I suppose to make it work, you have to pull this thing here…" pondered Sam.

He pulled the trigger, squirting Norman in the face!

"Sorry, Norman!" laughed Sam. "Just went off in my hand!"